Disney • Pixar's classic film *Toy Story* was released in 1995, the first ever feature film to be made entirely with computer-generated imagery (CGI). The film was nominated for three Academy Awards®, including a writing award—the first for an animated film. *Toy Story's* popularity and universal acclaim has resulted in two box office smash sequels: *Toy Story 2* and *Toy Story 3*.

A Gift For: William

Happy 3rd Birthday.

Love

From: Grandma Marg.

Published by Hallmark Gift Books,
a division of Hallmark Cards, Inc.,
Kansas City, MO 64141
Visit us on the Web at Hallmark.com.

Editorial Director: Delia Berrigan
Editor: Jennifer Snuggs
Art Director: Chris Opheim
Designer: Scott Swanson
Production Designer: Dan Horton

ISBN: 978-1-59530-533-6
BOK1224

Printed and bound in China
OCT12

Disney · PIXAR
TOY STORY

Hallmark
gift books

Woody the cowboy was Andy's favorite toy. He lived in Andy's bedroom with Slinky Dog, Rex the dinosaur, Mr. Potato Head, Hamm the pig, Bo Peep, and all the other toys.

And like all other toys, Andy's toys came to life!

One day, Woody called all the toys together. "Staff meeting, everybody! Andy's birthday party's been moved to today!" Andy and his family were moving to a new house soon and his mother wanted to have Andy's party beforehand.

The toys were worried. A birthday party meant new toys. What if Andy liked his new toys more than he liked them?

"What if Andy gets another dinosaur? I just don't think I can take that kind of rejection!" groaned Rex.

"Hey, listen, no one's getting replaced," Woody promised. "This is Andy we're talking about."

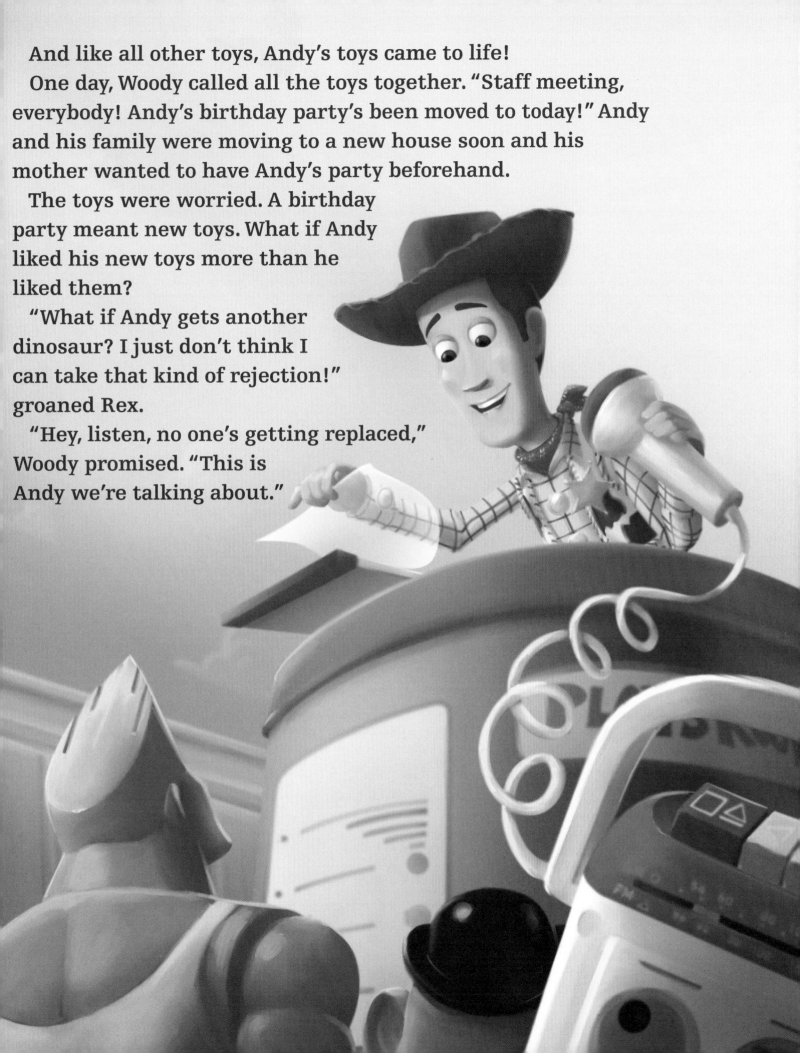

As Andy unwrapped his presents, the toys waited nervously. Everything was all right until the very last present—a flashy spaceman action figure. Andy brought the toy to his bedroom and went back to his presents.

"I'm Buzz Lightyear, Space Ranger," the newcomer greeted the other toys.

"He's *not* a space ranger," Woody scoffed. He turned to Buzz and said, "You are a *toy!* You *can't fly!*"

Buzz soon became a welcomed toy in Andy's bedroom. Everyone thought Buzz was wonderful. Everyone, that is, except Woody. Woody was jealous!

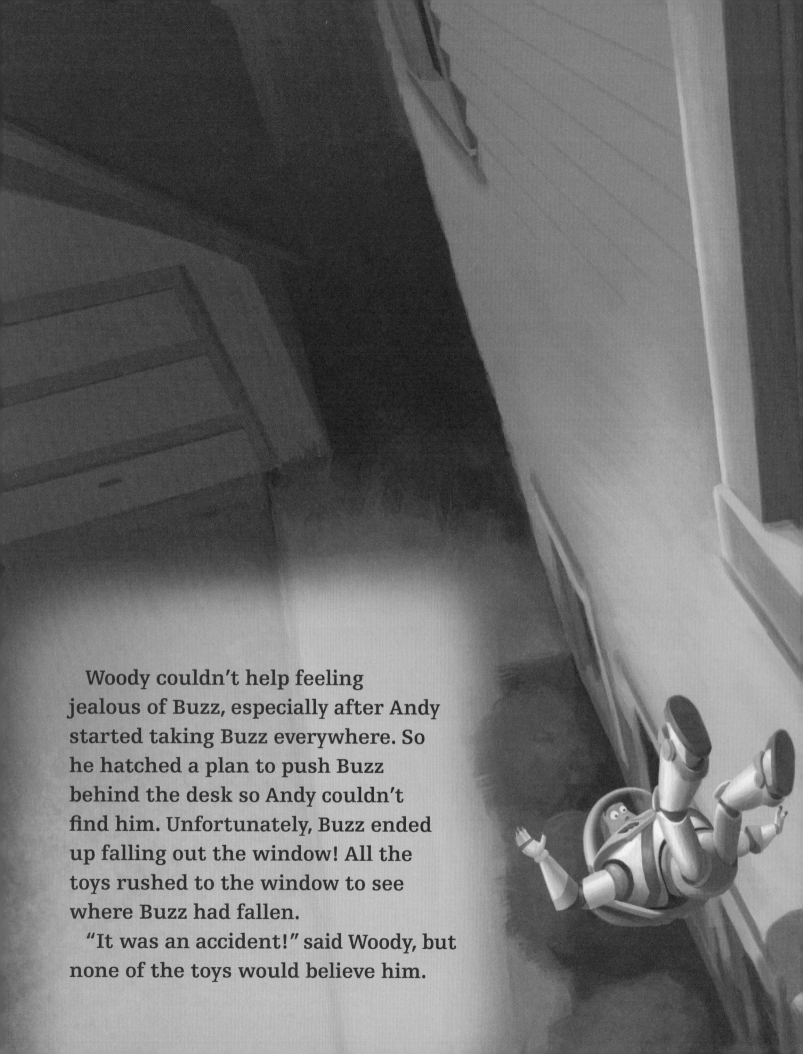

Woody couldn't help feeling jealous of Buzz, especially after Andy started taking Buzz everywhere. So he hatched a plan to push Buzz behind the desk so Andy couldn't find him. Unfortunately, Buzz ended up falling out the window! All the toys rushed to the window to see where Buzz had fallen.

"It was an accident!" said Woody, but none of the toys would believe him.

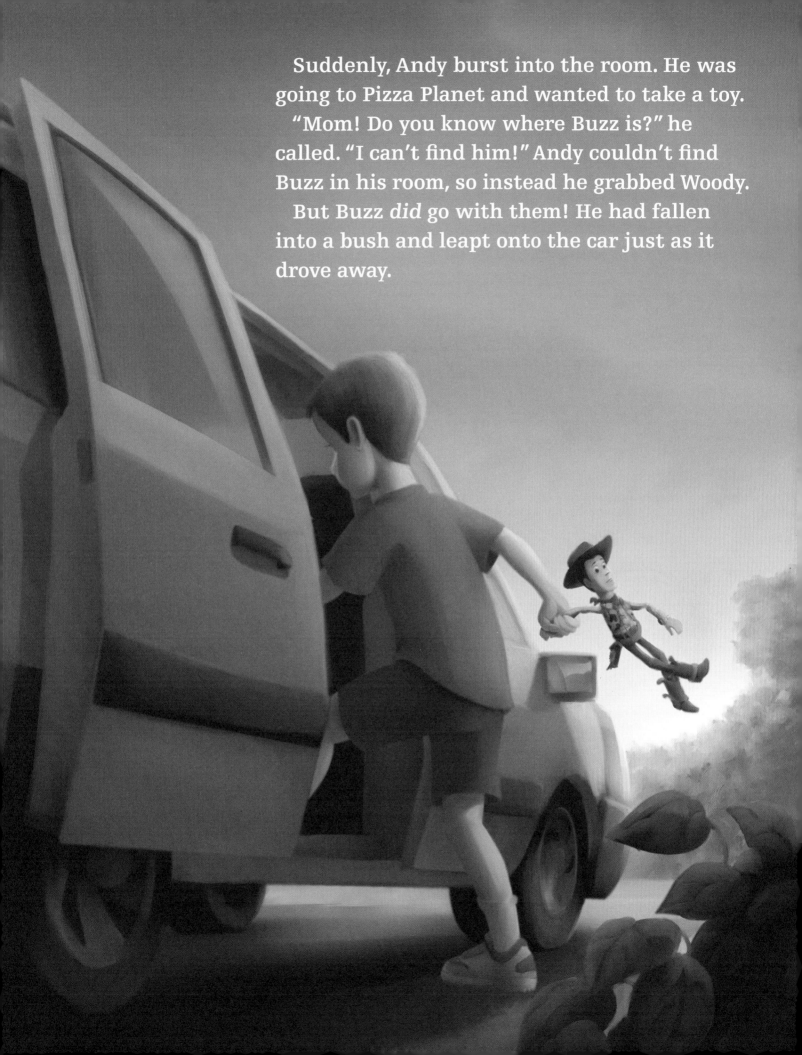

Suddenly, Andy burst into the room. He was going to Pizza Planet and wanted to take a toy. "Mom! Do you know where Buzz is?" he called. "I can't find him!" Andy couldn't find Buzz in his room, so instead he grabbed Woody. But Buzz *did* go with them! He had fallen into a bush and leapt onto the car just as it drove away.

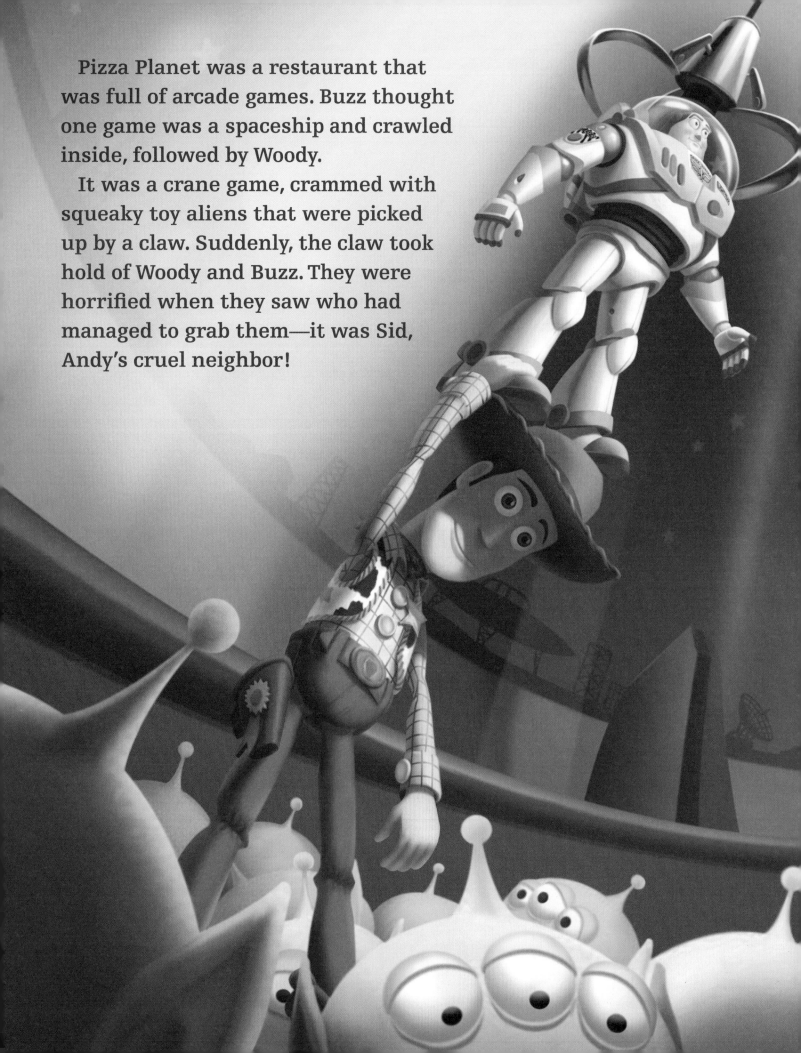

Pizza Planet was a restaurant that was full of arcade games. Buzz thought one game was a spaceship and crawled inside, followed by Woody.

It was a crane game, crammed with squeaky toy aliens that were picked up by a claw. Suddenly, the claw took hold of Woody and Buzz. They were horrified when they saw who had managed to grab them—it was Sid, Andy's cruel neighbor!

Sid carried his toy winnings
back home and up to his bedroom.
Woody and Buzz were terrified. They
were surrounded by weird-looking
mutants that Sid had made from toys
he had broken and then rebuilt in
strange ways. The mutants crawled
closer and closer toward Woody
and Buzz.

"Back! Back, you savages!"
cried Woody.

Buzz and Woody were just about to escape Sid's bedroom when Buzz heard a voice calling: "Come in, Buzz Lightyear! This is Star Command."
Buzz left Woody hiding in a closet and ran toward the voice, but it was only a television commercial for the Buzz Lightyear toy.
Buzz was stunned.

Desperate to prove he was a real space ranger, Buzz tried to fly. But he crashed to the floor, breaking his arm.

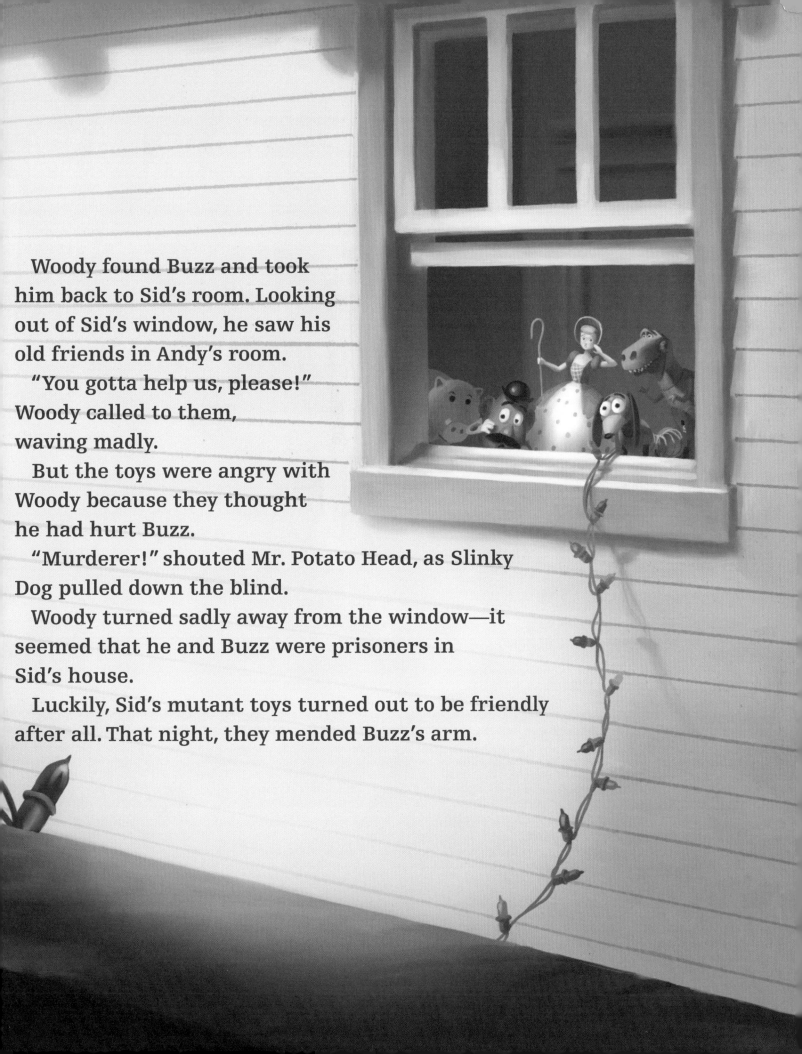

Woody found Buzz and took him back to Sid's room. Looking out of Sid's window, he saw his old friends in Andy's room.

"You gotta help us, please!" Woody called to them, waving madly.

But the toys were angry with Woody because they thought he had hurt Buzz.

"Murderer!" shouted Mr. Potato Head, as Slinky Dog pulled down the blind.

Woody turned sadly away from the window—it seemed that he and Buzz were prisoners in Sid's house.

Luckily, Sid's mutant toys turned out to be friendly after all. That night, they mended Buzz's arm.

Later on, Sid burst into the room. He grabbed Buzz and tied a big rocket to his back. "Yes! I've always wanted to put a spaceman into orbit," he laughed. "To infinity and beyond!"

That night, Buzz was sad and gloomy. "You were right all along," he told Woody. "I'm not a space ranger. I'm just a toy."

"Whoa, hey. Being a toy is a lot better than being a space ranger," said Woody. "In that house is a kid who thinks you are the greatest, and it's not because you're a space ranger, pal, it's because you're a toy. You are his toy."

Buzz thought for a moment and realized that even as a toy, he was an important part of Andy's life. "Come on, Sheriff," he said at last. "There's a kid over in that house who needs us!"

But it was too late! Sid's alarm clock rang. Sid reached out and picked up Buzz.

"Oh, yeah! Time for lift-off!" he said. He rushed downstairs and into the garden where he started to build a launchpad.

Woody turned to Sid's mutant toys for help.

"Please! There's a good toy down there. I've gotta save him, but I need your help!" he begged them. "He's my friend." The mutant toys smiled at Woody and nodded. Together, they worked out a plan to rescue Buzz.

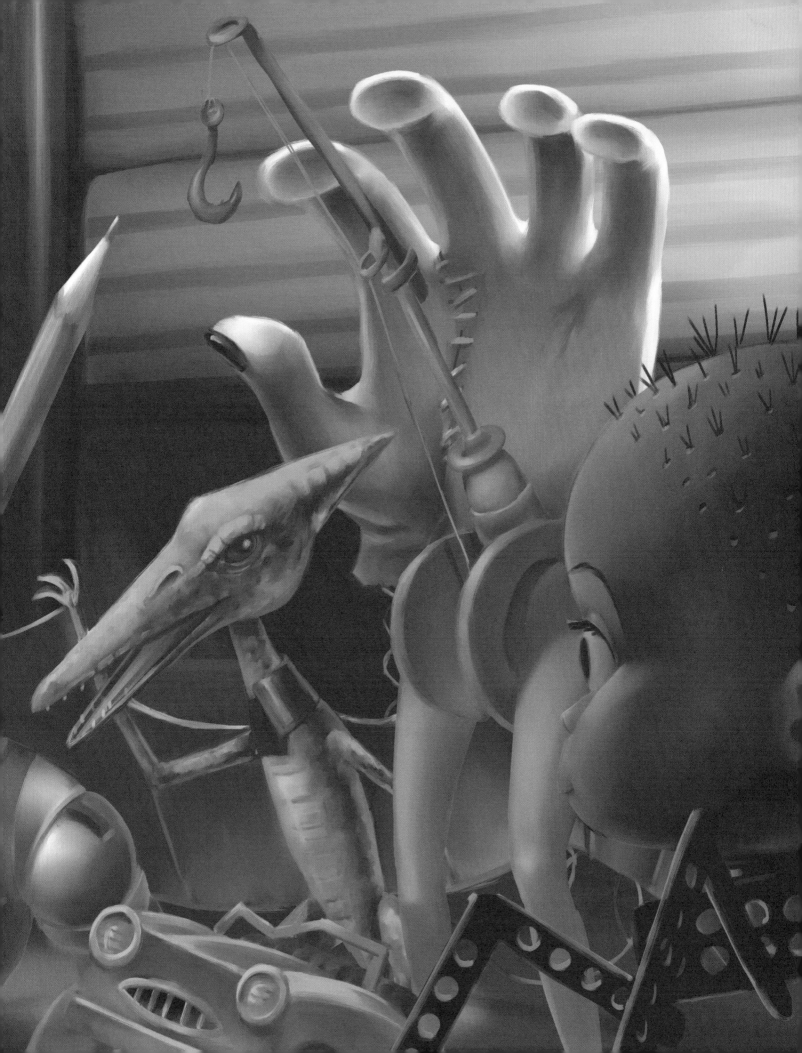

Out in the garden, Sid was ready to light the fuse on Buzz's rocket. "Ten! Nine! Eight..." he counted down.

Suddenly, Sid spied Woody on the ground. As he picked up the cowboy, his other toys crawled out and surrounded him. Then Woody spoke...

"We don't like being blown up, Sid, or smashed, or ripped apart..."

"Aaaaagggghhhh!" yelled Sid.

"From now on, you must take good care of your toys."

"The toys! The toys are alive!" Screaming, Sid ran into the house.

Woody and Buzz were free! They thanked the mutant toys for their help and began to make their way home, but Andy's family was just driving away, followed by a moving van!

"Woody! The van!" gasped Buzz.

"Quick!" yelled Woody.

The two friends rushed after the van. Buzz managed to climb onto the van's back bumper, but Sid's nasty dog, Scud, caught Woody.

"Get away!" shouted Woody, trying to free himself. Scud growled louder.

Bravely, Buzz leapt off the bumper and trapped Scud in a circle of cars. Now Woody was on the van—but Buzz was stranded on the road!

Woody scrambled into the moving van and found the box that contained Andy's toys. They were amazed to see him!

"Buzz is out there!" Woody told them. "We've gotta help him!" He grabbed the remote control car and sent it speeding down the street.

"Toss him overboard!" cried Mr. Potato Head, who didn't know Woody and Buzz had become friends. Shouting angrily, the toys threw Woody out of the van.

But a moment later, the toys' shouts turned to gasps of amazement as they saw Woody and Buzz come zooming toward them in the remote control car.

"It is Buzz!" said Bo Peep. "Woody was telling the truth!"
Then their car slowed down almost to a stop.
"The batteries! They're running out!" howled Buzz.
The car came to a stop and Woody and Buzz watched miserably
as the van disappeared into the distance.
Suddenly, Buzz remembered something. "Woody! The rocket!"
he yelled. Sid's rocket was still tied to his back!
They lit the fuse, and the rocket carried them up into the sky.

Just before it exploded, Buzz pressed a button on his chest. Out popped his wings, freeing them from the rocket.

"Hey, Buzz! You're *flying!*" laughed Woody, as they soared over the van.

Seconds later, they dropped gently through the sunroof of Andy's car.

Woody and Buzz were safe—and they were back with the boy who loved them.

After their adventures, Woody and Buzz became firm friends. Woody no longer felt jealous of Buzz, and the space ranger was happy to be a toy like everyone else. They all settled down together in the new house, and the next few months passed happily for everyone.

Christmas came and snow fell thick and soft
outside the house. Andy ran downstairs to open
his beautifully wrapped Christmas presents.

Once again, the toys watched for the arrival of
new toys.

"You aren't worried, are you?" asked Woody.

"No," replied Buzz. "Are you?"

"Now, Buzz," laughed Woody. "What could Andy
possibly get that is worse than you?"

The answer came as an excited bark.

"Wow!" laughed Andy. "A puppy!"

If you have enjoyed this book
or it has touched your life in some way,
we would love to hear from you.

Please send your comments to:
Hallmark Book Feedback
P.O. Box 419034
Mail Drop 215
Kansas City, MO 64141

Or e-mail us at:
booknotes@hallmark.com